No T. REX in the Library

by **Toni Buzzeo**

illustrated by **Sachiko Yoshikawa**

MARGARET K. McELDERRY BOOKS
New York   London   Toronto   Sydney

To Emma, with love and thanks for her perfect Eureka! moment
—T. B.

To Mela, Max, and Maya—S. Y.

MARGARET K. McELDERRY BOOKS

An imprint of Simon & Schuster Children's Publishing Division

1230 Avenue of the Americas, New York, New York 10020

Text copyright © 2010 by Toni Buzzeo

Illustrations copyright © 2010 by Sachiko Yoshikawa

All rights reserved, including the right of reproduction in whole or in part in any form.

MARGARET K. McELDERRY BOOKS is a trademark of Simon & Schuster, Inc.

For information about special discounts for bulk purchases, please contact Simon & Schuster Special Sales at 1-866-506-1949 or business@simonandschuster.com.

The Simon & Schuster Speakers Bureau can bring authors to your live event. For more information or to book an event, contact the Simon & Schuster Speakers Bureau at 1-866-248-3049 or visit our website at www.simonspeakers.com.

Book design by Debra Sfetsios

The text for this book is set in Softie.

The illustrations for this book are rendered in mixed media (colored pencils, gauche, markers, acrylics, soft pastels, and collage).

Manufactured in China

10 9 8 7 6 5 4

Library of Congress Cataloging-in-Publication Data

Buzzeo, Toni.

No T. Rex in the library / by Toni Buzzeo ; illustrated by Sachiko Yoshikawa.—1st ed.

p. cm.

Summary: A rampaging *Tyrannosaurus rex* demonstrates to an out-of-control little girl the results of "beastie" behavior in the library.

ISBN 978-1-4169-3927-6 (hardcover)

[1. Behavior—Fiction. 2. Libraries—Fiction. 3. Tyrannosaurus rex—Fiction. 4. Dinosaurs—Fiction.] I. Yoshikawa, Sachiko, ill.

II. Title.

PZ7.B9832No 2010

[E]—dc22

2008012142

1010 SCP

It's Tuesday morning in the library.

"ROAR!"

Tess is out of control.

"TIME OUT!"

Mommy shouts.

"No **beastie behavior** in the library."

Tess **snarls.**

She **snorts.**

"Just ten quiet minutes,
Little Beastie," says Mommy.

"And then I'll be back for you."

BAM!

Books tumble,

topple,

flop on the floor.

"**OOPS!**" Tess says. "The books . . ."

"ROAR!"

She gasps and grins.

She grips a claw.

And then . . .

T. Rex zips through the children's room.
Tess **bumps** along on his back.

"**Yee-haw!**"

Tess cheers.

Readers **scatter** in the wild clatter
of the history books tumbling down.

"**Watch out!**" Tess shouts.

"**The books . . .**"

Now knights in gleaming armor
lay siege,
hoisting their flags
and wheeling their steeds.

"Charge on,"

Tess trumpets.

T. Rex **tilts** and **whirls** through the door.

"Wait!" Tess shouts.

"The books . . ."

Water **spills** as the story pit fills with fish and aquarium treasures.

Orcas spout high.
Swordfish, jellies,
and squid reel by
the knights doing
synchronized swimming.

T. Rex **cannonballs** through them all . . .

. . . and bubbles up guarding the treasure.

A swashbuckling pirate surfaces nearby,

brandishing a hook for a hand.

"Arrr!

Return me booty, scurvy dog."

T. Rex escapes through the
Wild West display,
stomping past books on the floor.

"Be careful!" Tess cries.

"The books . . ."

Wild West

A posse of cowboys **gallops up** off the pages, their lassos **atwirl** overhead.

T. Rex **reels** through sagebrush and books. **Cattle stampede at his heels.**

"Take care!" Tess pleads.

"The books . . ."

T. Rex **thrashes**

and

trashes

Grabbing masses and mounds and

he builds

Earth & Science

the shelves.

mountains of books,

an escape to the stars.

From M to Mars—

"Please don't," Tess whispers.

From J to Jupiter—

"No! No!" Tess exclaims.

From S to Saturn—

"**Please stop.**

They're ripping!" she begs.

And on to . . .

RIIIIIIIIIIII

"TIME OUT!" Tess shouts.

"You're out of control!" Tess growls.

"No beastie behavior
with my library books."

T. Rex **fidgets.**

He **fusses.**

He **flings** out his tail.

BAM!

Books tumble.

topple,

flop

on the floor.

"ROAR?"

Tess **pushes** and **pokes** him.

She presses him **into his book.**

"Just ten quiet minutes, Little Beastie,"

Tess whispers.

"And then I'll be back for you...."